Noah's Ark

"Oh dear!" sighed Noah, "God said I should have two each of every kind of animal on board the ark. But I can only find one monkey! Where has the other one gone?"

God had told Noah to build the ark so that he and the animals would be safe from the great flood that was to cover the earth.

Can you help Noah find the lost monkey? You will have to go up and down the ladders and visit many different animals on the way. Use your pen to trace the route.

Can you see the dove? What did it bring Noah?.......
Do you know?

1 Was the ark 150ft, 300ft or 450ft long?

_____

2 How many people were in the ark? _____
3 Where did the ark come to rest? _____
4 What sign did God give that there would never be
another great flood? _____

You will find the answers in Genesis, chapters 6-9.

Where did Jonah go?

God wanted the prophet Jonah to take a message to the people of Nineveh. Jonah, however, did not want to go to Nineveh. He bought a ticket on a ship bound for Spain, instead. But when the ship was far out at sea, a great storm blew up and Jonah was thrown overboard!

What happened next? These five pictures tell the story, but they are all mixed up. Can you sort them out and put them in the order in which they happened?

Clue: The pictures spell a name.

O N

H J

The picture opposite of JONAH AND THE WHALE and its reflection, look the same, but there are 20 differences. Can you spot them?.......

You can read more about this story in the book of Jonah.

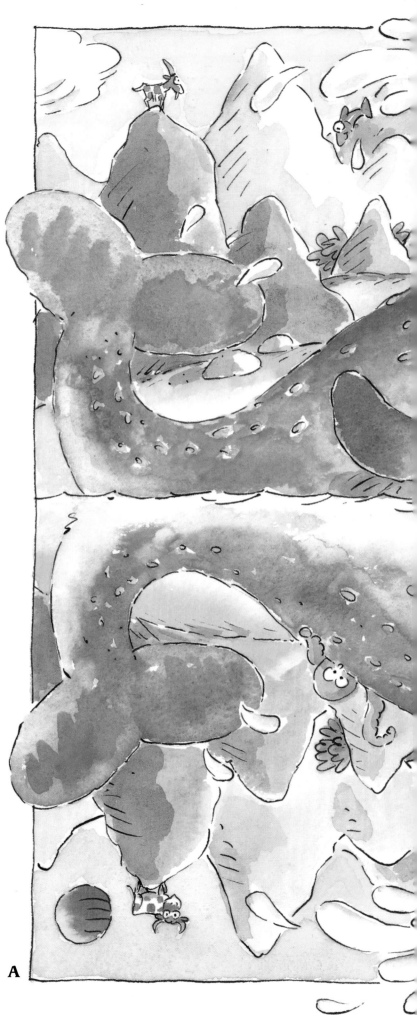

A

David and Goliath

"Ho, ho!" shouted Goliath, the big, bad giant. "Give me a man to fight!"

But everyone was too scared to fight Goliath. Everyone, that is, except David.

"I shall fight the giant," said David.

"You?" cried the king. "But you're only a boy!"

Can you work out what happened next? Sort out the picture strip-story and put it in the right order.

Clue: When they are put together correctly, the letters spell the King's name..

U

G

N

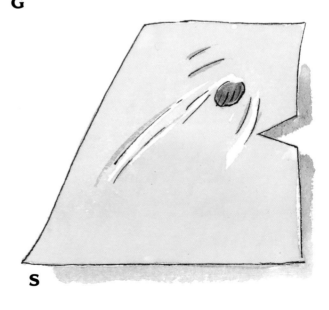

S

INCHES 1 2 3 4 5 6 7

L

A

Test yourself:

1 How many feet tall was Goliath?
Clue: 1+3-2+4+3 = _____ feet
(You can use the ruler at the bottom
of the page to mark out the height of
the giant.)

2 What did the king want David to
wear? A bullet proof vest, his armour
or his crown? _____

3 How many stones did David collect?
Was it 2, 5 or 7? _____

4 What weapon did David use to fight
the giant? Was it a sword, a gun or a
sling? _____

If you get stuck, you will find the story
in 1 Samuel, chapter 17.

K

I

| 9 | 10 | 11 | 12 |

Daniel and the lions

Daniel prayed to God every day. He worked hard for the king and was soon to be made governor over the whole kingdom. But the palace officials were outraged.

"Why should Daniel be over us?" they cried, and they persuaded the king to pass a dreadful new law:

"Anyone found praying to any god or man, except to the king, SHALL BE THROWN TO THE LIONS!"

So the next day, when Daniel prayed to God, the wicked officials arrested him and threw him to the lions!

The king was very upset. In the morning he hurried to the lions' den and peered inside. Then he cried out in surprise and jumped for joy.

Do you know why the king was so happy? Connect the numbers to find out.

When Daniel had been pulled out of the lions' den, the king made another new law. Can you work out what it says?

If you need any help, you will find the story in Daniel, chapter 6.

| DANIEL FROM |

| PRAY TO | GOD SAVED |

| DANIEL, BECAUSE | THE GOD OF |

| EVERYONE MUST | THE LIONS! |

Write the new law in the colored boxes below.

· BIBLE BRAINTEASERS ·

BIBLE BRAINTEASERS (Old Testament) is a wonderful introduction for young readers to five of the best-known Old Testament stories: *the Garden of Eden; Noah's Ark; Jonah and the Whale; David and Goliath* and *Daniel and the Lions.*

Fun and informative, this delightful book will captivate children with endless happy hours looking for the snake in the Garden of Eden ... chasing Noah's lost monkey ... unjumbling names and messages ... and lots more.

These pages can be wiped clean if you use a water-soluble felt-tip pen or a wax crayon. Other types of pen/pencil/crayon are not recommended.

This edition published by Victor Books/SP Publications, Inc.
in association with Hunt & Thorpe
Copyright © 1996 Hunt & Thorpe Ltd
Text © 1996 Linda Parry
Illustrations © 1996 Alan Parry
Originally published by Hunt & Thorpe 1996
Typography by Jim Weaver Design

Printed and bound in Italy

VICTOR BOOKS
A Division of Scripture Press Publications Inc.

ISBN 1-56476-573-3
90000

9 781564 765734

Children ages 5-9   6-3573

The stable

One day, God sent the angel Gabriel to a young woman named Mary. The angel told Mary that she would soon have a baby boy.

"He will be the Son of God," said Gabriel, "and you must name Him, Jesus."

Not long after, Mary and her husband, Joseph, went on a long journey to Bethlehem. But when they arrived in the little town, the inn was full and there was nowhere for them to stay.

"Never mind," said Joseph, "we shall sleep in the stable." And that night, baby Jesus was born! Mary wrapped Him in a blanket and laid Him to sleep in a manger.

Soon, some shepherds heard the wonderful news and came to visit the little Lord Jesus.

This picture of the nativity has some missing pieces. Find which piece fits in where and complete the star with your pen.

You can read more about the birth of Jesus in Matthew chapter 1, verses 18-24 and Luke, chapter 1, verses 26-38 and chapter 2, verses 1-20.

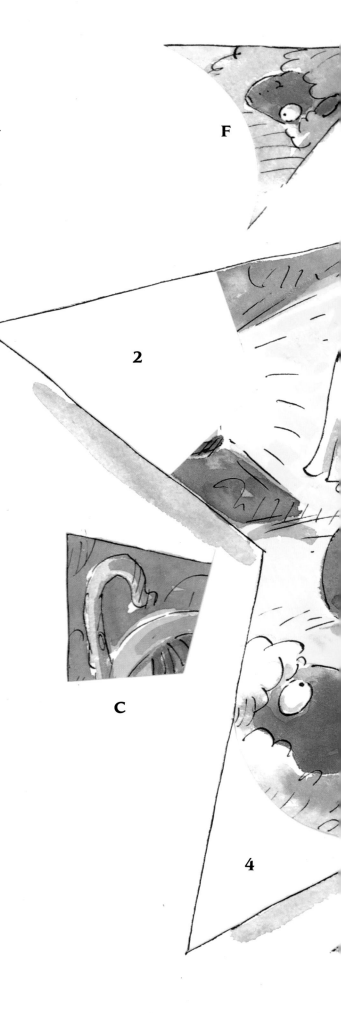